Welcome to AL

If you are looking for fast, fun-to-read stories with colorful characters, lots of kid-friendly humor, easy-to-follow action, entertaining story lines, and lively illustrations, then **ALADDIN QUIX** is for you!

But wait, there's more!

If you're also looking for stories with tables of contents; word lists; about-the-book questions; 64, 80, or 96 pages; short chapters; short paragraphs; and large fonts, then **ALADDIN QUIX** is *definitely* for you!

ALADDIN QUIX: The next step between ready to reads and longer, more challenging chapter books, for readers five to eight years old.

**Read more ALADDIN QUIX books
featuring Geeger!**

GEEGER THE ROBOT

PARTY PAL

BY
Jarrett
Lerner

ILLUSTRATED
BY
Serge
Seidlitz

ALADDIN QUIX

New York London Toronto Sydney New Delhi

ALADDIN QUIX
Simon & Schuster Children's Publishing Division
1230 Avenue of the Americas, New York, New York 10020
First Aladdin QUIX paperback edition February 2022
Text copyright © 2022 by Jarrett Lerner
Illustrations copyright © 2022 by Serge Seidlitz
Also available in an Aladdin QUIX hardcover edition.
All rights reserved, including the right of reproduction in whole or in part in any form.
ALADDIN and the related marks and colophon are
trademarks of Simon & Schuster, Inc.
For information about special discounts for bulk purchases, please contact
Simon & Schuster Special Sales at 1-866-506-1949 or business@simonandschuster.com.
The Simon & Schuster Speakers Bureau can bring authors to your live event. For
more information or to book an event contact the Simon & Schuster Speakers Bureau
at 1-866-248-3049 or visit our website at www.simonspeakers.com.
Book designed by Karin Paprocki
The illustrations for this book were rendered digitally.
The text of this book was set in Archer Medium.
Manufactured in the United States of America 1221 OFF
2 4 6 8 10 9 7 5 3 1
Library of Congress Control Number 2021941923
ISBN 9781534480261 (hc)
ISBN 9781534480254 (pbk)
ISBN 9781534480278 (ebook)

For Bodie, Dylan, Harper,

and Jaxon

Cast of Characters

Geeger: A very, very hungry robot

DIGEST-O-TRON 5000: A machine that turns the food Geeger eats into electricity

Tillie: A student at Geeger's school, and Geeger's best friend

Albert Einstein: Tillie's dog

Ms. Bork: Geeger's teacher

Gabe, Suzie, Arjun, Olivia, Sidney, Mac, Roxy, Raul: Other kids in Geeger's class, and also Geeger's friends

Contents

1

The Best Thing

Geeger is a robot. A very, very hungry robot.

Geeger was built by a team of scientists, then sent to a town called Amblerville. There, Geeger eats all the food that the rest of the townspeople don't want.

Rotten eggs, moldy bread, mushy fruit—those are just a few of Geeger's favorites!

Geeger has a brain, just like you. But Geeger's brain doesn't look like yours. His brain is made up of wires.

Most of the time, Geeger's brain tells him to do just one thing:

EAT! EAT! EAT! EAT! EAT!

At the end of every day, Geeger plugs himself into his **DIGEST-O-TRON 5000**. The machine sucks up all the food that Geeger has eaten and turns it into electricity. The electricity then helps power Amblerville. TVs turn on, dishwashers run, and micro-waves whir—all thanks to Geeger!

Geeger used to get confused and

DIGEST-O-TRON 5000

eat things he wasn't supposed to, like forks and batteries and toaster ovens. But ever since he became a student at Amblerville Elementary School, Geeger has gotten much better at eating only the spoiled and rotten and stale and expired food that he's supposed to.

But that's not the best thing about school.

The best thing about school is **TILLIE**!

Tillie is Geeger's best friend in the whole entire Milky Way.

She's smart.

She's funny.

She's kind.

She always knows what to do and say to make Geeger feel safe, **content**, and comfortable.

Seeing Tillie is always Geeger's favorite part of the day.

But today, Geeger is *extra* excited to see Tillie. Because today is Tillie's birthday!

Even better: **today is Tillie's BIRTHDAY PARTY**!

Geeger has never been to a birthday party before.

Tillie told the bot what to expect, though. There will be music and decorations, games and activities and snacks. And then, after all the games have been played and all the activities have been completed, Tillie and her guests will all sit down and eat birthday CAKE.

Just thinking about eating gets Geeger feeling hungry. And since he knows it's not a good idea to eat cake on an empty stomach, Geeger heads into his kitchen and fixes himself some lunch.

2

Albert Einstein

Geeger's lunches are nothing like *your* lunches.

You, for instance, might have a sandwich for lunch.

You'll get a couple slices of fresh, *non-moldy* bread.

Maybe you'll spread some nice, *non-expired* mustard on one slice, and some yummy, *non-expired* mayonnaise on the other.

Then you'll add some lettuce: a few crispy, not-at-all *slimy* leaves.

Then perhaps a thick slab of firm, not-at-all *mushy* tomato.

And finally, some cheese. A wedge of sharp, not-at-all *stinky* cheddar. A hunk of **mellow**, orange-edged—but not at all *green* or *moldy*—Muenster. And a gob of soft, slightly tangy—but not at all *nasty*—**Brie**.

Sounds tasty, right?

Well, here's what *Geeger* eats for lunch:

- 11 slices of bread (so moldy they're more green than brown)
- two jars of spicy brown mustard (expired)
- half a jar of Dijon mustard (super expired)
- three jars of honey mustard (<u>SUPER</u> expired)
- seven onions (mushy, and stinky enough to be smelled by Geeger's neighbors)

Geeger smooshes the last of the disgusting onions into his stomach,

then pauses in his eating. He wonders what Tillie is doing *right now*. . . .

Has she finished with the decorations?

Has she decided exactly what games she and her guests will play?

Has she gathered all the materials for the activities they'll do?

Geeger considers all of this for a moment, then he catches sight of the mountain of spoiled and rotten and stale and expired food heaped before him, and he gets back to his lunch.

He eats:

- six heads of lettuce (each of them slimy enough to be mistaken for a giant mutant slug)
- one enormous gob of Brie (extremely expired, and stinky enough to be smelled by Geeger's neighbors' neighbors)
- four bags of barbecue-flavored potato chips

(so old they taste like bits of barbecue-
flavored cardboard)

Geeger gathers up the last handful of chips and dumps them atop
the lettuce and Brie in his belly.
He's about to grab a bit more food—
but before he can get his fingers
on another **morsel**, his thoughts
bounce back to Tillie.

Or, to be more specific, Tillie's *dog*.

Albert Einstein. That's Tillie's
dog's name. (Tillie named him
herself!) He's a tiny guy with wiry,

black-and-silver hair that sticks out in all directions.

Geeger has only met Albert Einstein once. Tillie brought him over to Geeger's house while they were out on a walk. The dog ran right up to Geeger, licked his foot, rolled around in his flowers, then zipped and zoomed all across the lawn.

Albert Einstein moved so fast it made Geeger's wires hum and buzz like never before. Tillie had to hold on to the bot to keep him from toppling over.

It was WONDERFUL!

Watching the dog gave Geeger the same sort of giddy feeling he got when spending time with Fudge the Hamster, his class's pet.

Geeger was already plenty excited

about Tillie's party. But now, thinking about Albert Einstein being
there, he's *WILDLY* excited.

Quickly, Geeger finishes up his
lunch.

He eats:

- 37 pickles (expired and unnaturally sour)
- six avocados (barely green, mostly brown)
- one container of three-bean dip (older
  than old, and stinky enough to be smelled
  by Geeger's neighbors' neighbors' neighbors'
  neighbors)
- two packages of chocolate pudding (expired)

Geeger scoops the last of the pudding into his tummy. Then he closes the door to his stomach and checks the clock. And he sees that it's time to go.

Finally!

"TILL-*eee*'s birth-day PART-*eee*...," says the bot, **"here I COME!"**

3

Fancy Boxes

Geeger steps outside and into the bright sunlight. He **peers** up at the sky. It's a bold, beautiful blue—like it was just colored in with a brand-new marker.

There are a few clouds here and there. But they're white and fluffy, and, if anything, they make the blue of the sky even more vibrant.

In other words: it's the PERFECT day for a birthday party.

Geeger gets walking.

He's about a block away from his house when someone calls out to him.

"Geeger! Hey, Geeger! Wait up!"

Geeger spins around and spots **Gabe**, one of the kids in his class.

Gabe runs over, then holds his hand up for a fist bump.

"**HEL-LO**, *Gaaabe*," Geeger says, tapping Gabe's hand with his own.

As he does, he notices that Gabe is carrying something. It's a box, just about the same size as the bins that

Geeger and Gabe's teacher, **Ms. Bork**, keeps the class's art supplies in. But this box is unlike any box Geeger has ever seen. It's covered in some kind of shiny paper. The paper has green and blue stripes, and every time Gabe moves, it shimmers in the sunlight.

"**I LIKE** *your* **FAN**-*cee* box," Geeger tells Gabe.

For a second, Gabe looks confused.

Then he says, **"Oh!"**

He holds up the shiny green-and-blue-striped box.

"Yeah," says Gabe. "My sister helped me wrap it."

Geeger wants to ask Gabe what the box is for.

But before he can, his friend says, "Are you excited for Tillie's party or what?!"

And thinking about his best friend's birthday party, Geeger forgets all about Gabe's box.

"YES!" Geeger exclaims. "I have NEV-*errr* been so EX-cit-ed BE-*fooore*."

Gabe opens his mouth to say something else. But before he can get a single **syllable** out, someone else calls out.

"Geeger! Gabe! Over here!"

Geeger and Gabe look up the street. There, they see **Suzie**, another kid from their class.

As they make their way over to Suzie, Geeger sees that *she's* holding a fancy box too. Suzie's box is longer and thinner than Gabe's. And it's wrapped up in a different kind of shiny paper. Suzie's is purple and has little drawings of orange cats all over it.

Geeger finds it a bit odd that both of his pals are carrying these boxes. But this time, before he can open his mouth and ask about them, Suzie opens hers and shouts:

"I AM SO, SO, SO EXCITED!"

"*Same,*" says Gabe.

Once again, Geeger forgets all about the boxes.

"IF it is TILL-*eee*'s PAR-*tee* you are EX-cit-ed a-BOUT," he says, "then I am SO, SO, SO EX-cit-ed a-BOUT it *tooo.*"

Suzie throws her head back and looks straight up at the sky. "Can you believe this day?" she says. "It's *perfect* birthday party weather!"

"I know," Gabe agrees.

Suzie looks back down. She eyes Geeger and Gabe, and her mouth stretches into a great big grin.

"Well," she says, "what are we waiting for?"

Then, without any warning, she spins around and **sprints** down the street.

"FIRST ONE THERE GETS THE BEST SLICE OF CAKE!" she calls back.

"WHAT?!" hollers Gabe. "*TILLIE* GETS THE BEST SLICE OF CAKE!"

"THEN THE *SECOND*-BEST SLICE OF CAKE!" Suzie shouts, just as she turns a corner and disappears behind a house.

Geeger and Gabe share a look.

"You heard her," Gabe says. He tightens his grip on his shiny green-and-blue-striped box. "Let's go!"

Together, Geeger and Gabe take off, sprinting and giggling the whole rest of the way to Tillie's house.

4

Ruff-ruff-ruff!

Geeger and Gabe slow their steps as soon as they reach Tillie's front lawn. There, they see **Arjun** and **Olivia**, a couple more of their classmates.

Right away, Geeger notices that

they are holding fancy boxes too. Arjun's is small enough that he can hold it in one hand and is wrapped in *super* shiny gold paper. Olivia's is a little bigger and is wrapped in plain white paper that it looks like Olivia then used markers to draw on.

"Let's go!" Olivia tells Geeger and Gabe. "I think the party is around back."

Olivia leads the way, with Arjun and Gabe right behind her. Geeger, however, hangs back a few steps.

It feels like the wires in his head

have been **tangled** up in a great big knot.

Because, he realizes, something is up with these fancy boxes. There must be a reason why all of Geeger's classmates have brought one to Tillie's party. Is Geeger supposed to have brought one too?

He decides to do what Ms. Bork tells him to do whenever he's confused about something: He'll ask!

Geeger makes this decision just as he rounds the corner and catches sight of Tillie's backyard.

And what a sight it is!

There's a giant banner that shouts **HAPPY BIRTHDAY, TILLIE!** in enormous orange letters.

There are balloons—big ones, small ones, and in-between-size

ones—of every color of the rain-
bow.

There are tables **jam-packed** with
bowls that are overflowing with
snacks.

Chips!

Pretzels!

Popcorn!

Cheese puffs!

Candy!

Geeger thought he was already
as excited as he could possibly be.
But the sight of all that food some-
how gets him even MORE excited.

He can practically feel his circuits sizzling!

"Geeger! Geeger!"

It's Tillie. She's standing with her mom and dad, who smile and wave at Geeger. Tillie's dad gives her hair a tousle. And then she takes off, rushing over toward Geeger.

"TILL-*EEE*!" Geeger cries. **"HAPP**-*EEE* **BIRTH-DAY**!"

Tillie jumps into the air, does a twirl, and then takes a bow.

And just then:

"Ruff! Ruff! Ruff-ruff-ruff!"

Albert Einstein **bolts** over, moving so fast he's like a little **squiggle** of silvery-black lightning. The dog pauses long enough to give Geeger's leg a lick—"Hee-hee!" giggles Geeger. "That TICK-*ulls!*"—and then he's off again, zooming by the snack tables and zipping past the guests.

Geeger watches the dog for a moment, then turns back to Tillie.

"You're right on time," she tells her friend. **"The games are about to begin!"**

With that, Tillie takes off across the yard, swatting at a bundle of balloons on the way.

Geeger hurries along after her, the fancy boxes and his questions about them as far from his mind as can be.

5

Party Time!

The next hour is one big wonderful birthday party blur.

First Tillie grabs a huge orange tub and, turning it upside down, dumps out her entire collection of jump ropes. Gabe, Suzie, **Sidney**, and **Mac** all grab regular-size ones, then hurry off to a corner of the yard to see how many jumps in a row each of them can do.

Tillie, meanwhile, digs through the pile of ropes and pulls out a super long one.

Seeing it, Geeger can't help but think back to his first day of school.

He had mistaken a rope just like the one Tillie is now holding for an enormous strand of spaghetti and had almost *eaten* it. Geeger smiles, thinking about how far he's come since then. He can hardly

even remember the last time he ate

something he wasn't supposed to.

"Come on!" Tillie says, skipping

over to an empty patch of grass.

Geeger follows, as do Arjun and

Olivia. **Roxy** and **Raul** do too, but

then decide that they'd rather do

some chalk drawings on Tillie's patio.

And so Geeger, Tillie, Arjun, and Olivia take turns whipping the long jump rope around and jumping over it. When, that is, Albert Einstein doesn't get in the way. The pup keeps rushing up and trying to sink his teeth into the **revolving** rope, like *he* thinks the thing might be an enormous strand of spaghetti!

Once the kids have had enough of that, they pause for a snack break. Geeger tries a handful of pretzels and a handful of chips. Neither is stale nor expired. But they're still pretty delicious.

More games are played after that. First hopscotch, then Simon Says, then Pin the Tail on the Unicorn, followed by a **spontaneous** contest to see who can do the longest headstand.

Geeger takes part in the first two games, but sits out the third. Instead of trying to Pin the Tail on the Unicorn, he hangs out by the snack table, watching his friends have a blast and sampling the popcorn and cheese puffs and different varieties of candy.

Albert Einstein, finally tired from zipping and zooming about, joins

Geeger. He plops down at the bot's feet and sinks into a nap.

Geeger reaches down to give the pooch a pat on the head just as Suzie shouts, **"Okay, everyone!** Gather around! You know what time it is!"

Geeger looks at his friends. They're all grinning and nodding, like they *do* know what time it is, and like they are seriously excited about it.

But Geeger is seriously *confused*. He doesn't know what time it is. He looks all around, and he can't even see a clock!

Geeger lifts
a hand to get
Suzie's **attention**.

"Yeah?" Suzie
says when she
spots him.

"I am a-FRAID
I do NOT *knooow* what TIME it is,"
Geeger says.

Geeger's friends all share a look,
and their grins grow even bigger.

Then Suzie tosses her arms over
her head and screams, "It's time for
Tillie to open her presents!"

6

Presents?

"PREZ-ints?" Geeger says.

The word slips oddly through Geeger's wires. He's not sure he has ever heard it before.

"What are PREZ-ints?" he asks aloud.

But Geeger's friends are darting across Tillie's yard, and no one can hear him over the **commotion**. They're running, Geeger sees, toward their shiny, neatly wrapped packages. Someone piled them all up in the corner of the yard, near Tillie.

"I think mine's the biggest!" Roxy shouts, dragging a **humongous** package out of the pile. She lifts the thing over her head and gives a roar as the box's shiny silver paper sparkles in the sunshine.

"I made my wrapping paper myself," Olivia says. She shoves her prettily decorated package into Tillie's arms.

"See," she says, pointing out some of the things she drew. "That's a drawing of me. That's a drawing of you. And *that's* a drawing of Albert Einstein."

Tillie giggles.

"It's so good!" she tells Olivia.

"Open mine first!" says Gabe, setting his green-and-blue-striped box atop Olivia's. "You're gonna love it!"

"Mine second," Suzie says, placing her box atop Gabe's.

"Then mine!" says Arjun, placing his box atop Suzie's.

"Then mine!" says Mac, standing on his tiptoes so he can place *his* box atop Arjun's.

Tillie giggles again, and before all

the boxes fall to the ground, she sets them down. **Rearranging** them, she grabs Gabe's and carefully peels off the green-and-blue-striped paper. Next she opens the box—and her face lights up.

"Is this . . . ?" she asks, removing a small loop of bright, rubbery plastic.

"Yep," says Gabe, **puffing** his chest out with pride. "Your favorite jump rope. The one that snapped last year. I found it in my garage, then cut it up and glued the pieces together to make bracelets. There should be enough for everyone." Gabe lifts an eyebrow and grins. "Now, is that the best present ever, or what?"

"It's an amazing gift," says Tillie, slipping one of the jump rope bracelets over her hand and onto her wrist.

Gift.

Geeger hears the word—and the wires in his brain fizz.

Because *that's* a word he knows.

Does *present* mean the same thing as *gift*?

It certainly seems like it.

Was Geeger supposed to bring a
gift for Tillie?

It seems like it, too.

"UH-OH!" says the bot.

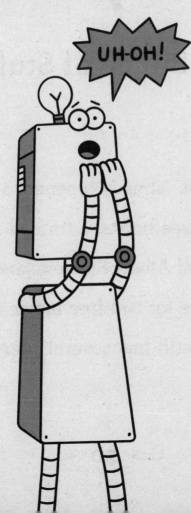

7

A Bunch of Stuff

Tillie has already opened a video game, three books, a framed picture of her and Albert Einstein, and a gift certificate for two free movie tickets. But she still has several presents to open.

Which means Geeger has some time.

He just needs to hurry up and figure out what to do.

Because Geeger finally understands that he is the only guest who didn't bring Tillie a gift!

What if she gets upset?

What if she thinks Geeger doesn't care about her or her special day?

Geeger can't let that happen.

But really, what can he do?

It's not like a birthday present is just going to all of a sudden appear

beside him. It's not like
gifts ever just fall out
of the sky.

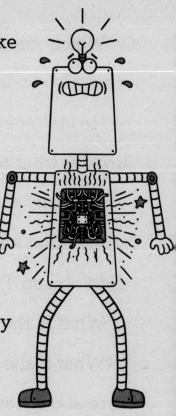

Geeger twists
his head this way
and that, looking
for something—
anything. The battery
in his chest begins
heating up. His
circuits start **misfiring**. Not even on
his first day of school did he feel this
overwhelmed and worried.

Tillie continues working her way

through her pile of presents. She's opening Raul's, after which she'll have just *two* left.

While his friends are still **distracted**, Geeger sneaks out of sight. He hides in Tillie's driveway, which runs along the side of her house.

What is Geeger supposed to do?

Should he leave?

Would that make things better or worse?

Geger doesn't know. All he knows is that he needs to do something— and **FAST**!

Standing there, as unsure as he has ever felt, Geeger spots a recycling bin. In it, there's a box! It doesn't have anything in it—but it could be a start.

Geeger grabs the box, the battery in his chest already cooling down. Next to the recycling bin, he sees a **scattering** of rocks. He picks through them until he finds one that kind of, sort of, if you squeeze your eyes shut just right, looks like the letter *T.*

Nearby, he finds a bright yellow flower poking up out of a crack in

the pavement. He plucks it from the ground and lays it and the rock in the box.

Around the front of the house, Geeger finds a few more things:

- a blue bottlecap
- a silver gum wrapper, twisted into a ring
- a pad of small pink sticky notes
- an orange marker with Albert Einstein–size bitemarks on the side

Geeger drops all the stuff into the box, shuts the top, then darts back up Tillie's driveway.

At the last second, he pauses by the recycling bin again. He digs a hand down into its **depths**, feels around, and yanks out a few pages of newspaper. He balls the paper up around the box and then hurries into the backyard and over to his friend.

"There you are, Geeger," Tillie says. "We were just wondering where you went."

"I was JUST get-*tinnng* THIS," Geeger says, presenting his present.

Tillie lifts an eyebrow as she looks at the big crumpled ball of newspaper.

"Is that . . . ?" she begins to ask. She leans to the side to study the ball of newspaper from another angle.

"Yes," Geeger tells her. "Your PREZ-int."

Tillie **hesitates**, but then accepts the ball of newspaper from Geeger. She reaches into it and pulls out the box. Smiling up at Geeger, she lets the newspaper fall to the grass below. Then she opens the box and peers inside.

Geeger watches as Tillie's smile slowly flattens. Then the corners of her mouth sag down into a frown.

Is she upset?

Disappointed?

Angry?

Geeger's worries begin to creep back.

"What is it?" asks Sidney, leaning over Tillie's shoulder to get a look inside the box, too.

"It looks like . . . ," says Gabe, " . . . like a bunch of stuff someone found on the ground."

The battery in Geeger's chest all of a sudden feels like it's hot enough to *melt*.

And then, just as suddenly, he's running.

Away from the party.

Away from his embarrassment.

Away from Tillie and her terrible, horrible frown.

8

Icing on the Cake

"Geeger? Geeger!"

It's Tillie.

She must have raced right behind Geeger when he bolted out of her backyard. Because he has barely made it to the end of the driveway, and here she is.

"Geeger . . . ," she says, looking up at the bot with a concerned expression. "Where are you going?"

Geeger lowers his eyes to the pavement. He finds it too hard to look Tillie in the eye.

"I . . . ," he says. "I did NOT get

you a PREZ-int, TILL-*eee*. I did NOT know I was SUPP-osed *tooo*. And NOW you are *saaad*. And may-BE ev-en *maaad*. And WORST of all . . . dis-ap-POINT-ed."

At this point, Geeger doesn't know what to expect from Tillie. But he certainly doesn't expect her to *laugh*. That, however, is exactly what she does.

Geeger can't help but lift his eyes and look at her.

"TILL-*eee*?" he asks. "WHY are you LAUGH-*innng*? You are

SUPP-osed to BE *saaad*. And may-BE *maaad*. And dis-ap-POINT-ed."

"But I'm *not*, Geeger," Tillie says. "I mean, presents are cool—sure. But they're not the real point of a birthday party. They're not even close to the best part."

Geeger lets all this information settle into his brain. Then he asks Tillie, "What is THE best *paaart*?"

"The best part is having all my friends over," Tillie says. "In the same place, at the same time. The gifts? Those are just like the icing on the cake. It's good and all. But even if it wasn't there, the cake would still be plenty awesome on its own."

The icing on the cake. This, Geeger realizes, is an expression, a figure of speech. Ms. Bork likes to use those. Geeger isn't sure he understand what this one means. But he thinks he might, and decides to try it out himself in order to see.

"It is LIKE the SNACKS," he says.

Tillie says, **"Huh?"**

"The CHIPS and PRET-zels and

POP-corn and *cheeese* PUFFS and CAN-*deee*," Geeger explains. "I *wiiish* they were ex-PI-*errred* and STALE. But EE-ven though they are *nooot*, they are STILL de-LISH-us."

This gets Tillie laughing again.

Geeger repeats the **phrase** he just learned, hoping to stick it more firmly in his memory: "The I-sing on the CAKE."

Tillie's smile slips into a grin. "Speaking of cake . . . ," she says. Then she takes off down the driveway, hurrying back to her backyard.

"Come on," she calls to Geeger.

Geeger goes after her. And just as he rejoins the party, Tillie's mom emerges from the house. She has a tray in her hands, and perched on the tray is an enormous cake.

All of Geeger's friends cheer when they see it. But not Tillie. She's too busy staring up at Geeger.

"Wait for it . . . ," she tells him.

"WAIT for WHAT?" Geeger asks.

Tillie points, and Geeger looks just in time to see his best friend's dad step out of the house. He's holding a tray, too. And on this tray is another cake. But it's no ordinary cake.

Even from all the way across the yard, Geeger can tell. It's **lopsided**. The top has **collapsed**. The frosting looks melty, the sprinkles more gray than rainbow-bright. The sight of it all makes Geeger's wires fizz and pop.

"We baked *that* cake last week," Tillie says. "Then we left it out in the sun for a couple days. The birds and squirrels started messing with it, so we had to bring it back inside. But it still got plenty nasty."

Geeger tears his eyes off the cake. He gazes down at Tillie. "It is . . . for ME?" he asks.

"Yep," she answers. "It's *all* yours. I don't think anyone else is going to want any."

Geeger turns back to the cake. His brain tells him: **EAT! EAT! EAT! EAT! EAT!**

And it's like Tillie can hear it. Because just then, she says, "Let's go, Geeger." She leads the way over to the table where her parents are carrying the cakes. "Time to eat!"

And eat they do. Geeger gobbles up his entire cake, and then even tries a slice of the regular cake that

all his friends are eating. It's not as good as his was—but it's not bad.

Not long after the last crumbs of cake have been consumed, the party ends. Geeger's friends start heading home.

Geeger is the last one to leave. He's just about to say goodbye to Tillie when Albert Einstein begins barking his head off.

Both Geeger and Tillie look and see the dog zipping around in excited circles.

"What is he so happy about?" Tillie wonders.

Finally, the dog stops long enough for Geeger and Tillie to see what he has in his mouth. It's an orange marker. The one Geeger had found in front of Tillie's house and given to her as part of his last-minute present.

Tillie laughs. "**The marker!** He's been looking for it all week," she says. She smiles up at Geeger. "I think you just made Albert Einstein's day."

A grin forms on Geeger's face. And just when he thinks *HIS* day can't get any better, the dog gallops over, leaps up into his arms, and gives him a great big lick.

Word List

attention (ah•TEN•shun): A person's focus

bolts (BOLTZ): Moves suddenly or quickly

Brie (BREE): A soft, mild, creamy cheese with a firm white skin

collapsed (kuh•LAPSD): Fallen or caved in

commotion (kuh•MO•shun): Noisy disorder

content (kuhn•TENT): Happy, at peace

depths (DEPTHZ): The place deep below the surface

distracted (dis•TRAK•ted): Not paying attention to something

hesitates (HEH•zih•taytz): Stops or pauses

humongous (hyoo•MUN•gus): Very large in size, enormous

jam-packed (JAM•PACT): Stuffed to overflowing, crammed in

lopsided (LOP•sigh•ded): Not straight or upright, crooked, uneven

mellow (MEH•lo): Mild in flavor

morsel (MOR•suhl): A small piece

misfiring (miss•FIHR•ing): Failing to work properly

peers (PEERZ): Looks closely at

phrase (FRAIZ): A part of a sentence

puffing (PUHF•ing): Expanding in size

rearranging (ree•ah•RAYNJ•ing): Changing the order of

revolving (ree•VAHL•ving): Turning or spinning in place

scattering (SKA•teh•ring): A group separated in all different directions

spontaneous (spon•TAY•nee•us): Something that is not planned

sprints (SPRINTZ): Runs at top speed

squiggle (SKWIH•guhl): A wavy line

syllable (SIH•lah•bull): One of the parts into which a word is divided to pronounce

tangled (TAYN•guhled): Twisted

Questions

1. Tillie loves to jump rope, which is why she and her friends jumped rope at her birthday party. What sort of activities do you hope to do at your next birthday party?

2. Gabe doesn't buy a birthday present for Tillie—instead, he makes one. Have you ever made a gift for someone? Can you think of a gift you *could* make for someone?

3. Geeger learns that the words *present* and *gift* can mean the same thing. Two words that mean the same thing are called "synonyms." Can you think of any other synonyms?

4. At the end of Chapter 7, Geeger feels embarrassed. Think of a time you felt embarrassed. Why did you feel that way? How did you react? What made you feel better?

5. In Chapter 8, Geeger learns the expression "the icing on

the cake." Can you explain what this expression means? Can you use it to describe a situation from your own life?

6. Tillie's dog, Albert Einstein, zips around in circles when he gets excited. What do you do when you feel full of excited energy?

CHUCKLE YOUR WAY THROUGH THESE EASY-TO-READ ILLUSTRATED CHAPTER BOOKS!

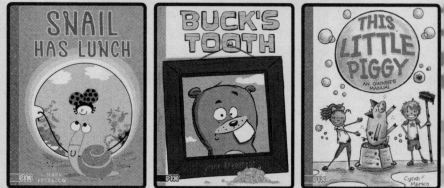